Let's Call Him
Lau-wiliwili-humuhumu-nukunuku-nukunuku-āpua'a-'oi'oi

Tim Myers

Illustrated by Daryl Arakaki

3565 Harding Avenue
Honolulu, Hawai'i 96816
phone: (808) 734-7159
fax: (808) 732-3627
e-mail: sales@besspress.com
http://www.besspress.com

Design: Carol Colbath

Library of Congress Cataloging-in-Publication Data

Myers, Tim.
Let's call him Lau-wiliwili-humuhumu-
nukunuku-nukunuku-apuaa-oioi / Tim
Myers ; illustrated by Daryl Arakaki.
p.   cm.
Includes illustrations.
ISBN: 1-57306-252-9
1. Fishes - Hawaii - Juvenile fiction.
2. Names, Personal - Juvenile fiction.
3. Hawaii - Juvenile fiction.
I. Arakaki, Daryl. II. Title.
PZ10.3.M993 2005   [E]-dc21

09 08 07 06 05   5 4 3 2 1

Printed in China through Colorcraft Ltd. Hong Kong

Audio CD recorded at Rendez-Vous Recording, Honolulu
Performer: Bill Sage
Production coordinator: Caryl Nishioka

Once in the waters of Hawai'i there was a triggerfish swimming joyfully and boyfully over the reef. He was a very proud fish, so he used his old Hawaiian name. He thought it sounded ringing, singing, kingly.

When he met other fish—tangs or tunas or squirrelfish—he would say, "I am the humu-humu-nuku-nuku-āpuaʻa. He said it slowly, syllable by syllable, so the other fish would hear it precisely, exactly, and indubitably. Then he would ask the other fish to say it back.

He was very proud of his shining long name, so he made sure the other fish knew how to say it precisely, exactly, and indubitably.

And so it was.

Now the sea is wide, and the reef is big, and there are as many fishes as there are stars in the night. There was another fish on the reef, swimming whirlfully and girlfully. She was a long-snouted butterflyfish. She was very proud too. Just like the boy fish, she used her old Hawaiian name.

When the conchs and seahorses and needlefish asked who she was, she would say, "I am the lau-wili-wili-nuku-nuku-'oi-'oi. She said it proudly. She loved the long surfy sound of it. She too made sure it came out right when other creatures said it— except for the cruising tiger sharks, of course, with whom she was quite shy.

And so it was.

One day a great knocking surf came rolling over the reef. The force of the green water threw the girl fish and the boy fish together.

They had never seen each other before. And since he was a finely colored fellow, all bluish, whitish, auburn, yellow, and ivory, and since she had the loveliest parrot-yellow body and a fine spindly snout, they liked each other. A lot. He felt a deep fishly feeling for her, and she felt swimmy just at the sight of him.

So they had a fish wedding, there on the pearly-light, sun-streaked bottom. The fishes all danced with their tails in the sand. And they ate breaker foam for wedding cake. Everyone was happy—especially the bride fish and the groom fish.

In time they had a fish child—and that was when all the bubble-bubble began.

The father fish said, "I am the humu-humu-nuku-nuku-āpua'a. This child is my child. It will be called The Child of the Humu-humu-nuku-nuku-āpua'a."

"But this is my child too," said the mother fish, "and I say it will be called The Child of the Lau-wili-wili-nuku-nuku-'oi-'oi!"

All the other reef creatures listened as the mother and father argued. Then the other creatures began to argue too.

"Why are YOU so proud?" the octopus said to the father fish. "Your name means you have the snout of a pig." Then the octopus changed the color of his skin to match the coral, which he often did when his feelings were strong.

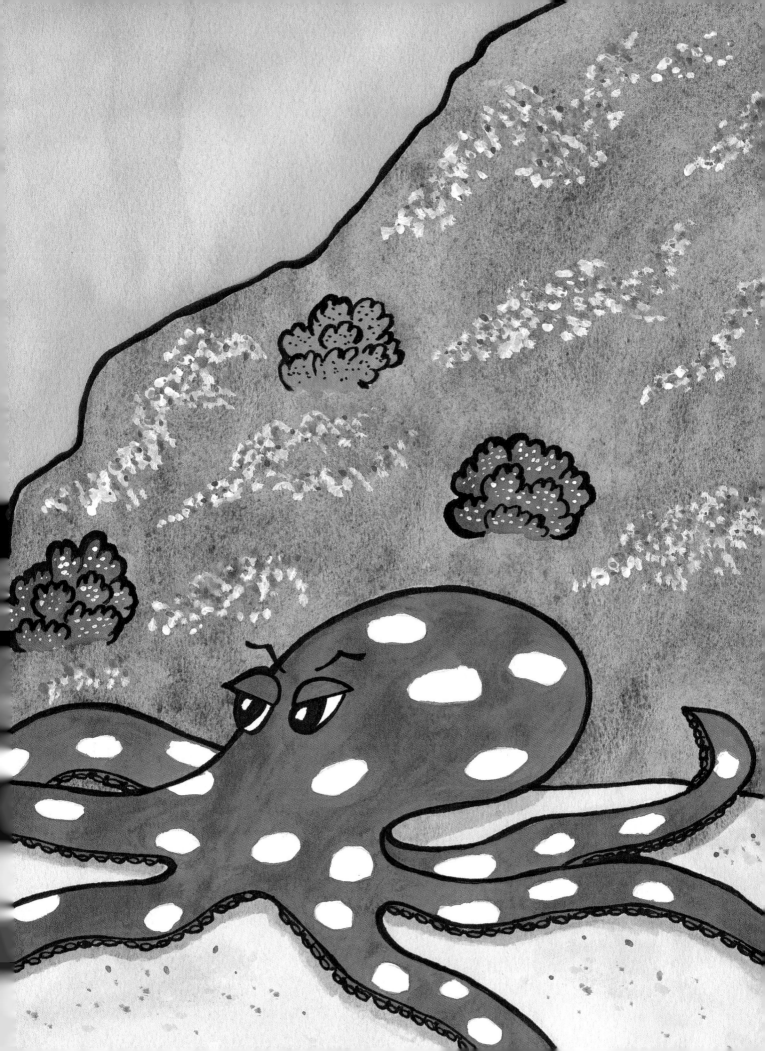

A little Christmas wrasse, colored
like a rainbow, asked, "What is a pig?"
"I don't know," said the octopus
bashfully, sinking into a hole.

"And why are YOU so proud of your name?" said a mahimahi to the mother fish. "It means you swim like a leaf blows around on a wili-wili tree. And you have a big nose." (This was extensively true.)

But the mother fish and the father fish each refused to give in. "You must go to Kihikihi, the Moorish idol!" shouted a parrotfish out of its birdlike beak. "She is the best fish of all. She will decide!" So they all went.

Now the reef creatures are very beautiful, and they think the Moorish idol is the wisest of them all, because she is the most beautiful (which is a silly thing to think, as you shall see). She is black and yellow and white, striped broadly up and down, and her upper fin is very long. It trails like a lovely flag behind her, rippling in the water as she swims. She looks like a queen of the fishes.

The reef creatures told her everything. "What shall they name the child?! What name?! What name?!" they asked, crowding their scaly and spiny and shelly bodies all together.

The Moorish idol swam slowly, slowly, with her little white fin-flag fluttering in the shift of the sea. After many waves had passed and crashed overhead, she finally spoke in a cool fishy voice.

"The child should be called . . .
Lau-huku-numu . . . . No, just a moment.
Lau-humu-humu-'oi-wili . . . . Let me try again.
Lau-humu-āpua'a . . . . No, no no. Hmmmm.
How about 'Oi-'oi-lau-nuku . . . ? Wait, wait—I know!
Perhaps it should be . . ."
And she said it all at once, in a gurgly rush:

"Lau-wili-wili-humu-humu-nuku-nuku-nuku-nuku-āpua'a-'oi-'oi!"

But by this time the reef creatures had already swum or crawled or skittered or glided away, and even the mother fish and the father fish had swum off together. They'd all decided to call the young one Hapa. That means Little Bit.

Hapa was very proud of his name. He
liked the bubbly short sound of it. And he
made sure everyone said it precisely,
exactly, and indubitably.
And so it was.